Coming Down Fast

And Other Sexy Encounters

Coming Down Fast

And Other Sexy Encounters

Kaysee Renee Robichaud

Twice Told Tales Press
Houston, TX
2019

Table of Contents

Coming Down Fast

And Other Sexy Encounters

Coming Down Fast

Roy tugged on one of the straps encircling Sally's shoulders, cinching it tighter than she had, and the effect was the same as pulling on a pet leash: an undeniable attention grabber. "Pop quiz," he said for the third time since takeoff. In lieu of an actual question, he indicated one of the lines on his chest, while the airplane's engines whirred and droned in the Jeopardy theme (the mile high techno-mechanical remix, Sally considered it after receiving so many pop quizzes).

The line in question terminated in a red and white handle, solid looking but not cumbersome. Anchor shaped for easy gripping and tugging. Impossible to ignore when needed. Sally pursed her lips. "The reserve chute line?"

"Outstanding," he replied. He was a good-looking man with brown eyes that could be gentle or stern as the situation demanded. His brush cut emphasized the smallness of his ears and the narrowness of his face. The hairstyle choice was a leftover of what he referred to as his "misspent youth" aboard one of the Navy's floating city aircraft carriers, but a secondary effect from those days was his attention to bodily discipline. He was still in prime fighting trim. He had broad shoulders that could wrestle loose rigging back in place even during high storms, solid arms that could bench two hundred easy, abs and ass tight enough to bounce back tossed change, leg muscles to kill for.

Sally knew she was pretty enough. And not in bad shape, either. She had her sights set on an MMA title, and that demanding exercise regimen weeded out the truly unmotivated. The slick magazines dedicated to her sport enjoyed her bad girl image, casting her as a dark-haired Veronica in a world of Betties, vying for world domination. They played up her height and her build, thankfully playing down the massive ankles she had always hated. Those ankles were a leftover of her father's Scottish heritage, while the rest of her was classic Castilian Spanish beauty with an exotic touch of Syrian.

Headlines of late had been less about her body than the Thrash and Thunder bout this coming weekend, and though she was geeked to be on her way, she was also a bit terrified. The best solution for that? A little special something-something to celebrate six kinky months with the man who really understood her.

His suggestion had surprised her, all right.

"Tell me the routine," he said. Clipped words that were perfect for military leadership or for playing the top role in their bedroom/playroom.

Though the Short SC.7 Skyvan aircraft was a relatively small one, the lack of seats near the rear offered the illusion of space. It was still pretty cozy, and when the airplane heaved a little, she fell right into him. Roy being Roy, he caught her without so much as a grunt.

"You are in control," Sally said.

"Details, please." Though his manner was brusque, he was simply offering her the standard line that all parachuting professionals at Good To The Last Drop gave to their first timers. There were a lot of things to keep straight when performing this sport.

Good To The Last Drop's company literature referred to these as tandem jumps.

"You have control over the main and emergency chutes. I will be tied to you." The rigs were something right off www.ExtremeRestriants.com but made for more than play. Buckles and straps made from solidly designed synthetics and leather. Hers were tight across her torso, with lines that slung around her shoulders and beneath her breasts and between her legs. The world's tightest hug, comforting and compassionate. Just being in her current rig brought her warm squirmies. And soon she would be strapped back-to-belly against her man, and then the two of them would be plummeting through the air together, hoping that the primary or emergency parachute would work. "We go out together, and we arrive together. My life is in your hands. You," she repeated, "are in control."

He flushed with power as she said this again, color burning across his pale cheeks and forehead. He glanced back toward the cockpit, separated from this rear area by a flimsy looking sheet stretched across a curtain rod. Roy had called this "the privacy veil," and explained that it was a mostly ineffective barrier between the crew and the folks, which allowed those mind-changers to "bitch out without 100% embarrassment." Of course, the crew would know when they landed, but there was no real razzing. The shame was born internally. "Cowards die a million times before their deaths," Roy had upped Shakespeare's famous line, "the valiant taste of death only once. And even then, we miss out on the flavor."

"You," she said a third time," are in charge."

Most of her life was spent being the killer queen. In the ring, in the gym, in her 9 to 5 team management gig at the zoo. She had to make decisions, plan out not only her own life but those of people around her. It was a relief to find someone worth giving her trust to.

Like Roy.

"I want you to suck my cock," he said.

"Here?" Her eyes shifted from his to the curtain. Timmy could peek back at any time. "Now?"

"You ever thought about joining the mile high club?" he asked.

When she had been lying in bed with him last Monday, talking about the coming bout and the low level background worries, which had resulted in this surprising skydiving suggestion, she had originally been thinking Roy was asking her to join the ranks of that particular club. Sure, the twin prop they were in was not quite a mile up, but it was close enough for her. However, Roy was firm in his assertions that "Flying at approximately 4000 feet, was nowhere near the 5,280 feet measurement of the according to NIST-OWM mile."

NIST, he had helpfully supplied when her face corkscrewed with confusion at the acronym, stood for the National Institute for Standards and Technology, whose Office of Weights and Measures served as some kind of measurement uniformity authority. She imagined them as a bunch of police officers armed with measuring tapes instead of Tasers, and this made her smile.

The mile high club … did they even have time? They were up here to jump, not get jumped.

Although …

"And who is in control?" His voice was a deep growl. The kind of thing that made her already quivering parts thrum with joy.

In response, she ran her hands down his chest, across his own harness. The bulge below was all Roy, and it was a pleasant treasure to find. Though he was belted in, nothing was close to constricting his junk. That would be a bad idea when the chutes were deployed, he had explained, and the retarding jolt would tug every line to a halt.

His cock was rock hard and ready, and she knelt before him as she freed his shaft. Took that meaty banana's familiar curve between her lips and deep as deep could be. His manhood tasted wonderful, now that they were blood bonded.

She teased him with short strokes and a playful tongue, and he moaned softly for her, trembling and shivering when she wanted him to. Oral sex was not a duty, it was a pleasure. The way Roy got off on her efforts got her off, too. Her body responded to him, sympathy passion.

His hands were firm on her neck and back, playing with her through her clothes. Solid strokes. She took him all the way in, past the point of gag reflex, and a flood of saliva filled her mouth. She held him until the fires caught in her chest, and then she lost control of herself. A little choke pulled him deeper still and a touch of milk spilled down her throat.

Then, he pulled her head off his erection. His strong arms brought her to her feet and into a passionate kiss. While their mouths worked, he teased her back and then her breasts. Using her strap harness rig as he might use a spreader bar to drag her closer, to position her how he wanted.

Then, his fingers worked a little magic, showing her the actual reason he had suggested a certain style of pants. She had been surprised when he provided a pair of olive drab slacks for her. She was usually a fan of more colorful clothing. However, these had a special feature hidden under a cunning elastic patch: the zipper started just below the button and went down and around, stopping just short of the waistline in the rear.

These pants could transform from dressy to open crotch with a simple slip of the zip.

Which was what Roy was doing now.

"Mile high, Sally," he whispered. "Let's take it a mile high."

Her response was a throaty whisper. "Take me, Roy. Take me hard."

His cock was already there, and soon enough, so was the rest of him. He lifted her onto a stack of secured crates. Unzipped and legs spread, he had a nice view of her lacy black panties. Black, of course, because she was feeling naughty today. The lace featured little skulls and roses, a fun mix, but nowhere near as fun as the things his fingers were doing to her. Nudging and teasing and playing along her slit.

She nibbled along his throat, pausing to suck on his Adam's apple, and he replied by tugging her panties aside. Pushing his fingers into her warm, wet place.

Quickies were not usually her preference, but there was something special about the immediacy here. Something intensely erotic about his riveted attention and the clock ticking in the back of her mind. As well, something thrilling about the thin partition between pilot Timmy and their lust. *Will he even be able to look us straight in the eye after he lands?*

"Fuck me, Roy. Get that dick inside me."

He held her panties aside and teased her slit with his shaft. Rubbing it back and forth, sending tingles straight to her core. Then, he caught hold of her harness and pulled her tight against him. Onto him. Her response was louder than expected, an uncontrollable yelp of pleasured surprise.

Then, he was fucking her. Fast and frantic and perfect. Hotter sex than they had ever had, and the thermometer had broken quite a few times before. The harness was cinched tight around her, the straps confining and comforting. He used them to regulate her speed. When she wanted to go faster, he kept her steady. It drove her wild.

Then, she was coming on him, the smell of their sex flooding the rear compartment.

His hands and his mouth never stopped teasing her. She bit him hard enough to leave round teeth marks. It was amazing.

Suddenly, he was out, and she was turning around, and he finished opening the zipper, baring her ass. His shaft nudged the naughty hole, and she gritted her teeth. This would be rough, maybe even bad rough, but she wanted him. It would hurt like hell later, but damn it all *she wanted him.*

He kept her waiting. The clock ticked off almost twelve seconds in her head before his shaft sank home.

Slid right in without the expected friction burn. Only pleasure.

"Lubed," she squawked, surprised. He had slicked his shaft with some kind of lotion or gel. His firmness filled her ass so nicely. She moaned and shoved back against him, rubbing him. He again caught her by the strap harness rig, using this to control her motions.

"Faster," she pleaded, but he stayed steady.

"Harder," she whispered, but his constancy remained untouched, the denial thrilling her to greater heights still. She came again, keeping the verbal fireworks low and hopefully subtle. Then, he was pulling out of her and pulling her zipper shut before stowing his still engorged cock.

"You ready for the long ride down?" he asked as she straightened her gear.

There was no time for hesitation. No desire to change her mind. Their fucking had touched her somewhere deep, tapping that fear keg and letting the contents drain out. Replacing them, maybe, with something far more hopeful and helpful.

"You are in control."

He snapped clips between their harnesses. This pulled her in still new ways. His erection's bulge was positioned right behind her ass, and she momentarily imagined the two of them fucking all the way down.

Her system as overloaded with stimulation, the straps nice and tight, her warm and wet quim sending out happy vibes. He guided her to the door, checked their straps one more time.

"Remember to keep an eye on your altimeter."

Altimeter? What was that? Oh, yes. The thing on her arm. A gauge that resembled an analog watch with numbers in the thousands.

"Also remember," he said, "that I have you. You're strapped to me, and I've got you."

They did not seem like the most romantic words she had ever heard before, but right now? With only a slender piece of steel between them and 4000 feet of wind and nothing between them and the ground? They were quite romantic indeed.

She tried to say those three little words, but hesitated too long before starting. She got out the "I" but then the door opened, and the wind screamed before them, and they were jumping out of a plane.

Though Sally had subconsciously expected them to fall straight down, they actually moved parallel to the aircraft as well. They had been going over one hundred miles per hour on a straight trajectory, already. Residual momentum carried them forward and downward together descending along the latter half of an inverted parabola.

The world splayed before her like a gigantic map, individual farmlands to the north looking like patches on a quilt. The wind was a screaming, laughing thing. It took her a moment to realize the latter laughter came from herself. She was falling, in her head she knew she was, but her body just felt the push of the wind, felt the pull of the straps, and the presence of her man behind her, guiding them down, down, down.

The harness was better than bondage ropes or a corset. Hugging, comforting, controlling. The falling part — or gliding, or whatever it was they were doing — that was about loss of control. The two sensations built into an incredible mixture of panic and pleasure, and as Roy wiggled behind her, she caught just enough of the bulge in his pants to push herself further toward another climax.

Suddenly, she was coming at 4000 feet. Free falling into an afternoon delight. She screamed her orgasm into the wind. Her eyes were locked open, watching the world through her goggles, untouched by the raging winds. She felt like she was sliding down a snowy hill on a polished aluminum disc. Speeding, speeding gone.

Roy shifted again, and the straps pulled against her chest, her crotch, and another orgasm washed through her.

The world that was — one where she was worried about bouts and the future, her dreams and her destiny — winked out in importance, as her man guided them toward the steadily expanding patch of earth destined for their feet. She waved her arms, found the action not as easy as she was used to. But the thrill of pushing was fun.

The thrill of falling was amazing.

He would see them down. They would land safely, she knew. And when they did, she would be different thanks to a new perspective.

That was one thing —

Her straps eased a third orgasm from her.

— one thing this sort of activity granted. Perspective. The world was ultimately small; the people and all their problems were smaller still.

Her eyes managed to fix on the altimeter on her wrist. The needle was descending at a steady rate. All according to plan. All according to physics and the NIST-OWM, she supposed, who would monitor such activities and technologies with well-maintained measuring tapes and digital doodads.

She giggled, warm with this experience.

When the needle struck the right number, Roy pulled his cord and the primary chute opened without issue. Their descent arrested for an instant, and a fourth orgasm burst from her. She wanted to turn around. Cuddle close to this man, her fellow, her Roy.

The straps held her stable and fixed.

She was satisfied with that.

For now.

Her body was not quite done, though. They still had a couple of thousand feet to go, and her heart and pussy would have nothing less than coming down fast and hard. She screamed her wild, wonderful emotional overload to the heavens, to the waiting earth below.

Trussed Issues

When I said, "Tighter, please," the jerk tying me to the chair looked nearly apoplectic. His buddy's eyebrows rose so high that his forehead looked like corrugated steel. Whoever these men were, they apparently were not used to their kidnap victims asking for special treatment other than the "please let me go" variety.

I had been a really quiet girl after they tossed me in the trunk of their beat to hell Ford sedan and slammed the lid. Before that, of course I had been yelling my damned fool head off. Who really wants to be kidnapped?

Well, maybe I do. But not for realsies. Only for, you know, fake.

When they got me to the cluttered back woods garage destination, let me out of the trunk, cuffed my wrists together, tugged a hood on my head that smelled like chicken feed (not part of my fantasy life, but I do not judge others) and marched me to God only knows where, I was really, really quiet.

When in Stockholm . . .

My panties were already soaked. My traitorous little hoodie-below would not be swayed by the fact that these two goombas were trouble (capital T or otherwise). It was all kind of thrilling really. Especially since I had an ace in my . . . Well not an ace in my hole, which is also not a part of my fantasy life (paper cuts, anyone?), but I had an ace on my *side*.

The reason they had grabbed me, of course, was because of who I was. Gretchen Spanx—and if that name did not set me up for a bottom's life, I don't know what would—secretary to the one and only Eddie Seamus, the meanest, rudest, and yet most clean cut Private Eye in town. With a name like that, could he really be anything else?

What they didn't know was that Eddie had fired me only this morning. It was all part of the cycle. I cleaned out the liquor from his filing cabinet; he found out, blew his top (but not his load) and then fired me for a few days. At least until he filled up his filing cabinet again. A cycle as old as time, though apparently not public knowledge.

Eddie would eventually come for me. He was a bastard and could be a real sadist (my stars howdy, *could* he!), but we worked well together and I did not think he would leave me out to dry. Not me, his Faithful Gal Friday Night (or Sunday morning, since I was not all that good a church girl).

However, it would take him a while to notice I hadn't come back. And then it would take him a little while to catch wind that I had been abducted. And then it would take time for him to come to my rescue. In the meanwhile, I had to keep the palookas entertained so they didn't decide to act terribly unprofessional with me. Ungentlemanly.

A little tough knot love was a-oh-kay with me, but too rough could trade elsewhere.

So, when the two men marched me from the barn to their sticksville hidey-hole, I did not complain one bit. In bad circumstances, I figured a policy of Shut The Hell Up would keep me alive the longest. Our footfalls crunched across gravel, and I grew frantic worrying about my cute little shoes. Not very sensible, was I? My brain worrying that the white/black leather heels I had purchased only last week were already scuffed all to hell . . . Then, those palookas led me up three solid, wooden steps, across an uneven wooden porch, and through a creaky door.

I flashed back onto the last time I had been bound, blinded, and walked someplace like this. It had been two years ago, and the guy doing it had been The Putz I was dating, a tourist-top who stripped me to my fashionable undies, tied my wrists, pulled a Smiley Face pillowcase over my head, and then led me to a mysterious dwelling. Instead of carrying through with playtime, however, he tossed me in, slammed the door and ran away laughing. And he did not come *back*. When it stopped being fun, I played the old "Wriggle Until the Ropes Loosen" Game and finally pulled the hood off to see that I was stuck in the local haunted house. A pragmatist, I did not believe in ghosts, but I sure screamed my pretty little head off when I saw the tacky furnishings and . . . *choke* . . . the cockroaches creeping too close to my naked legs.

Well, I was furious and humiliated and the only person I could call, believe it or not, was Eddie. He picked me up and got the story out of me. He dropped me off at home and paid a call on The Putz What Did It. Broke The Putz's nose. Broke his jaw. Broke a couple ribs. I never knew he cared so much.

Eddie could be a sadist (*sigh*), but as things turned out he was *my* sadist. I knew he would come now.

So, when the kidnapping jerks got me inside, they pulled off the hood. Shock of shocks it was a cabin we were at. Probably one by Moose Lake, since we had not been on the road nearly long enough to get anywhere else. Outside, a loon called.

A chair waited. Uncomfortable looking and high backed. Around it, brand new rope. Not clothesline either; this was the real deal soft but strong stuff. The kind that kidnapping jerks would not be likely to use on someone they were going to rub out right away.

Well, my breath caught in my throat and my eyes just about filled with tears. Two strong looking tough guys, dragging little old me to a bondage cabin at Moose Lake? If my panties had not been wet already, they would have soaked through now.

There's something about ropes that, well, have always gotten to me. Even back in childhood, in the old neighborhood, when the guys wanted to play their macho Good Guy/Bad Guy games and let me hang around to be the Damsel in Distress, I talked them into tying me up for reals. And leaving me be for a while. A rope around the wrists is pretty reassuring, around the body is like a big old hug. And when someone leans down over you, and they have total power, well, there's something even more reassuring in that. Particularly if it's a safe environment, where the real power lies in the bound and "helpless" damsel.

So, when the two jerks marched me over, laughing like a couple of heavies straight out of some forgotten 1940s noir picture—

Timothy Carey wannabes—well, I was all atremble. My heart fluttered like a caged bird. Not because of fear but excitement.

All for those ropes. All for the power exchange. The *play*. They sat me down, and went to work.

And wouldn't you know? Their work was for crap.

The ropes weren't tight enough, the knots were sloppy, and the whole thing was sooo disappointing. Well, you can see why I slipped and said:

"Tighter, please."

"Did you say something?" Mr. Heartattack asked. He towered over six and a half feet, with shoulders wide enough to start a bar on.

I pouted, my lower lip pushing out and drawing a deep enough breath so my twin distractions could draw attention. "Sorry," I said.

Mr. Corrugated Head was a couple inches shorter, a foot narrower, but his hands were enormous. If he cupped one of those oven mitts over my mouth, it might pinch my nostrils shut and maybe block out my eyes. Perfect bondage hands, those were. He said "I think she's floiting with us, Barry."

That's what he said: *Floiting*. Flirting, I think he meant.

So, Mr. Heartattack was Barry.

"Don't use m'name, Joel," Barry said and then stopped the tie job to palm his forehead. Nice hands, but not so nice as his buddy's.

"Well, that's done," said Joel. I liked my names for them better. More evocative, less . . . ordinary. "Holy hell." Joel glanced up from my right side. "Lady, is that your panties I'm smelling?" He looked like someone had hit him with the smile shovel. So big a grin, I expected cartoon birdies to flutter around his head before he keeled over backward.

"Yes," I said, my pout deepening. Submitting to these two guys was too hot. My traitorous bits were getting even juicier.

"That's not pee is it." There was no question to this. We both knew we were smelling honey but not gold.

"No," I said, a little breathless. "It's not pee."

"This," said Mr. Heartattack (I mean Barry), "I've got to see." He reached down to my skirt and hiked it up. Flapping fabric across my chin. Baring my white silk panties, my thigh highs, my six strap suspenders.

How humiliating.

His tough guy tug turned my legs to water. The shame only turned me on even more.

"Damn," Barry said, "she gets any wetter, she'll flood the place." His laugh was the "yuck-yuck haw-haw" of a one trick crony.

"Well, we ain't gonna force you," Joel said, his forehead once more looking like corrugated steel. "Though I dunno if that's good news for you or bad?"

Barry asked "You like it rough, baby? You want to play bitch?" His unimaginative vulgarity told me all I needed to know about him: Barry was a douche bag as well as a jerk and a lousy knot tying schmuck.

"I don't want to be forced," I said. Not for realsies, anyway. Play was different. Play was, well, *play*.

"You finish tying her down," Barry said. "I need to take a dump." Mentally, I added tact to the list of qualities Mr. Heartattack did not possess. At least he left to do his business instead of popping a squat on the floor and letting fly like some subhuman. He had the sense to be housebroken.

Joel finished tying, and of the two he was the better knot man. Those hands of his. I could not stop staring.

"Why you looking at me like that?" he asked.

"Anyone ever tell you you've got great hands?"

He studied them, slowly turning them over. It was the best peep show I ever attended, watching those hands. "They don't seem too special," he said.

"But they're so," I said, panting a little, "*big*."

"I know," he muttered. "Makes finding gloves a real sonofabitch, let me tell you."

"I'll bet," I said, approving anyway. "But they sure are nice."

He got a little mischief in his eyes. "You like a guy with big hands? A doll like you?" He even talked like Timothy Carey, his teeth barely opening. It was weirdly sexy. I imagined Joel in black and white, mugging for the camera, and I had to admit the picture really worked for me. "Answer me honest," he said.

"I do. I like a man with big hands." The confession sent fresh shivers through my spine and fresh warmth through my pussy. "I like big fingers."

"To do a little something like this?" He put one hand over my mouth, and just as I predicted, it closed off my nose. His other hand clamped onto the back of my head. He stared into my eyes, and I stared into his, as heat built in my lungs. My chest was heaving, trying to draw in fresh air, but nothing came. I was completely in his power.

God, what a turn on.

He got a cruel touch to his grin, and I almost came right there.

I batted my eyelashes when it was getting to be too much. When the fireworks went off behind my eyelids. When the threat of unconsciousness crowded rational thoughts from my mind.

He let go, before I went out, and I drew in full, deep breaths. He watched my breasts rise and fall.

"You like that?" he asked, and I could tell he rather enjoyed doing it. "Answer me honest."

"Yes," I said and managed a smile. "That was fun."

"Your lipstick's all smeared," he said. His palm took a couple of turns across his pants leg. "I won't do that again."

"All part of the game."

"Game?" He looked puzzled. "You like rough trade?"

"Not like how Barry meant," I said. "But a little. Bruising's not my kink. But a little overpowering, a little . . . you know." I squirmed a little in the ropes, which slipped imperceptibly down. "I like being tied up good and tight."

"Tight, huh? Well, I like things a little tight, too." He gave me a wink. "But ropes aren't really my forte."

"I can tell."

"What's that supposed to mean?"

"You weren't an Eagle Scout," I said. But boys can be taught, when the carrot dangles in front of them. "I can show you how, if you want."

"You can show—" Confusion made a blank slate from his face. "Lady, don't you realize you been *kidnapped*?"

"I do," I said, "but I figure on making the best of it. You said you weren't going to force me. Was that honest?"

"It was."

"And I figure all this effort means you aren't going to whack me when you're done, right?"

Joel nodded. "You're right at that. We don't whack broads. I mean ladies."

"You can call me a broad," I said, feeling flush. "I'm your tied up damsel, aren't I?"

"You're a funny gal," he said. "A real funny gal." He was not laughing, however. Not even smiling. I had been called worse. "Show me, if you want to show me."

I wiggled and all the ropes pooled around the base of the chair. If I wanted, I could have gotten to my feet and run. He looked fairly dumbstruck at the ease with which I released myself.

I took him through the steps. I showed him how to double up on the cord, how to wind it around one of my ankles and one of the chair legs. I showed him how to make a good knot, not the limp grannies he had called satisfactory.

When the rope cinched tight but comfy, my body shivered with appreciation. "Damn," I said, "that feels good." To Joel, I said, "Now you try."

It took him a couple of attempts, but he started picking up the skill. I rewarded him with a delicious shiver and a coo. "Nice." Watching his hands was its own reward.

"Your arms won't be so easy," he said.

"Actually, you just worry about the wrists. Pull my arms behind the chair and bind the wrists together. When you're done with that, use a second piece around my chest. Should be able to go twice, once over my breasts, once under."

At mention of my bosom, he turned a deep red. It was a terribly precious response for such a tough guy.

He tied me down, and I soaked my panties all over. When he was done, he ran those big fingers of his along my cheeks, tender, and slipped his fingers between my lips. "Suck," he said, and I did. He got off on this, so I sucked harder. He stiffened and then excused himself.

Barry returned around then, and the party stuttered as it once again slipped back into low gear. "Look, Ms. Spanx. You don't have to worry none. We're just supposed to hold you to distract your boss from looking too close into what *our* boss is up to."

It almost made sense. I wasn't worried, however. "I do have some bad news for you, though."

"What's that?"

"I got fired this morning."

Barry blinked at this, not understanding. I must have gone outside of whatever tough guy playbook he was operating out of. Secretaries don't get fired in his little worldview, when in reality, assistants got fired all the time.

"It's true," I said. "When Eddie figures out I've been nabbed, he'll come looking all right. But that won't be until like next week."

"Shit," Barry said. "You've got to be lying."

"Not at all. I'm not saying he'll never come, I'm just saying if you want to use me like you're supposed to, you're going to have to hang on to me for over a week." I squirmed in the ropes. Nice. "Do you have enough food and such?"

"We got food coming out our asses," he said, charming me all over again. I made a mental note to never ask him a serious question again. "Water too. The Moose . . ."

Moose Lake. That was affirmed. As if on cue, another loon sang out. Or maybe it was the same one.

"Good," I said. "Because we're going to be sitting together for a while."

"I can't," he said. "I've got shit to do on Saturday. It's visitation. My ex- gets stingy for time, and I can't miss seeing my little bastard." How he could inject wistfulness into that particular pet name is a mystery to me to this day.

"Bring him out," I said. "Show him the ropes of the family business." Bad, I know, but it made me smile at the time.

"I don't think so, lady. I want him to be a lawyer when he grows up."

Genius, I thought. What better way to get out of the slam than to manufacture your own legal counsel? "Well, it looks like you might be sunk for that."

"Nuh-uh," he said. "I'm gonna talk to Gordon. He'll—" He blinked a few times, and then smiled. "I see what you're doing. You got me to say the boss's name. Very tricky for a frail."

He said frail. Can you believe it? Who uses words like that anymore?

"No you didn't," I said.

"I did. I said Gordon. But at least I didn't say Gordon Hewitt." Face, meet palm. Palm, meet face.

I suspected those two elements had a long history of coming together.

I said, "You did not just do that."

"You make me crazy, lady. You should be freaking out, or something. You shouldn't be pumping me for information."

"I'm not pumping you for anything! You're spilling your guts!"

"What's going on, out here?" Joel with the hands returned.

"Bitch says Eddie fired her this morning."

"The lady says what?"

"He did," I replied. "It's part of our little thing. Has to do with me dumping his stock of whiskey."

"You dumped his whiskey?" Barry asked, as though only mooning the Virgin Mary might be a worse offense. "How low is that?"

"If he really wanted to hide it," I said, feeling strangely defensive, "he wouldn't always put it in the same drawer in the file cabinet. He knows I can't stand that stuff!"

Joel asked, "He fired you?"

"If that's the worse he done," Barry said, "you got off lucky. Dumping a man's whiskey . . ."

"If she got fired," Joel said.

"Your boss's plan will have to wait until Eddie comes looking."

Joel said, "But you said he—:"

"He fires me regularly. And then he gets soft and comes looking for me."

The two men looked at me, all bound up, and their gazes were hungry. Made me horny all over again. There's something about being the center of attention that gets me incredibly hot. Throw some ropes in, and I'm sold.

"What the hell are we supposed to do?" Joel asked.

"Well, I can't babysit the doll all weekend," Barry sure sounded whiney. "I got shit needs doing."

"Well, then what?" Joel demanded. "It's not like we can let her go and then pick her up again next week, when Eddie Seamus will start looking."

"You got plans this weekend, Joel?" I asked.

"Me? Naw."

"Well, you could babysit me, couldn't you?"

He considered this. "Yeah," he said. I wriggled a little, and the idea sank in a little further. "Hell, you bet. Go see your kid, Barry. I got this all cinched."

Yeah, he said cinched. Groan along with me.

"You sure?" Barry asked.

"I'm sure."

"Okay then. It's settled."

Now both men looked at me with new curiosity. I could tell what they were thinking. How did this frail, this kidnap job, get so damned complicated? And how did this lady get the upper hand over us? I decided not to say anything more, just batted my eyelashes and wore a "Who, little old me?" face and savored the situation while it lasted.

I figured the playtime would not last terribly long. Eddie would not be distracted by me until next week, and while the two palookas realized this, their boss didn't. Their boss would probably act, and Eddie would get involved, and then discover my abduction.

Maybe someone even heard me screaming when they grabbed me. Maybe that someone even did the right thing and called for help.

I had only a brief amount of time to savor the bondage, so I might as well enjoy what I had.

The ropes become fast friends, reassuring and wonderful. When they came off, during those times I had to step into the water closet to pee or do the other, I did not feel a sense of freedom. Instead, I felt imprisoned. When I was roped, I was in charge. When I wasn't my two captors were in charge, and not in a good way. I counted down the hours, minutes, seconds to Friday.

When Friday finally came, I was giddy. Barry waited the whole blasted day before he left, not taking off until an hour before nightfall. After he was gone, Joel hunkered alongside me, put one of those gorgeous hands on my thighs and said, "Alone together at last."

To his credit, Joel did not rip my clothes off right then, right there. Instead, he played gentleman, which was charming and sweet. He made a light dinner of meat product dressed up with greens. After the microwave sounded the dinner bell, he dragged my chair over to a table so I could sit in the candle light. The emergency candles' glows played over his leathery face, his tough guy features. They softened nothing, but that was fine by me.

Joel fed me from his own fork, and held the straw for me to drink. He made things a little too easy, did not make me strain at all. "You can make me work for it a bit more," I said.

He looked like a big kid. Said he was sorry. After dinner, he showed me what kind of man he really was.

He dragged me back to where I had been parked. Halfway between the sofa and the wall. Clear view of the television, though I hated that damned box, and out of sight of the place's two big windows. He turned on some music and performed a striptease for me. I suspect he realized the big draw was neither his unskilled gyrations or his fumbles with buttons, belt and zipper, but the simple way his hands moved.

Those two massive things glided through the air, defying music and sometimes sense. They had a life all their own, and though the fingers were not used to performing in slow motion, they accomplished what they set out to do. After a few attempts.

When he stood naked before me, my breath caught in my throat. His body was a tapestry for scars of all sizes, but it was beautiful to behold. Muscled and toned by fire baptisms. His erection bobbed in the air before his six pack stomach like a mad conductor's baton.

I strained in my seat, and the tight ropes held me firmly in place. Oh God, it was glorious.

He sauntered toward me, those hands swishing through the air before him as though caressing a wheat field's bumper offerings. Hypnotic.

When Joel reached me, those hands of his touched my face. Running along my jawline and through my hair. Strong and not on speaking terms with gentleness. Bless his heart, he tried.

His smile was as crooked as his morals. His eyes were steely and hungry. His gaze was as undeniable as the ropes. His fingertips explored my mouth, and he said, "Get them nice and slick." I ran my tongue over them, running moistening laps.

Satisfied, Joel ran those wet fingers down. His dry hand wrenched my dress up, tugged my panties aside, baring me.

"Is this what you want?"

I was breathing too heavily to answer. I scooted my ass as much as I could to offer my sex.

"Tell me," he commanded.

When I was too slow in responding, he drew his wet fingertips along my pussy, dipping inside to tickle me at my most sensitive. "My God, yes, Joel, I want it."

"Tell me more," he said. "Tell me what you want me to do to you."

"I want you to touch me. Finger fuck me. Fist me."

His fingers found the way inside. Penetration was delicious and cruel. My body wanted to squirm, but the ropes kept me in place. Joel's lips crooked wider; he was a natural at this. I gasped when the first orgasm washed through me. Between the ropes and his hands, I got half a dozen more in twice many minutes.

His cock bobbed, eager.

"Fuck my face," I gasped.

He shivered, as though never once thinking about this.

"Now," I moaned. "Please."

He said, "Not yet," and I quivered. Joel's hands sped up, rubbing me in all the right ways along with a few of the wrong ones. It was easy to overlook the mistakes, he was so into the moment.

When his hand was slathered with my lust, he straddled me. "You want this, now?"

"Joel," I said.

"Open up, if you want this."

His engorged cock was the sort of thing a sculptor might envision as the perfect complement to those hands. Sizeable and veined.

Obediently, I gazed up at him with my best little girl lost expression and let my lower jaw drop through three jittering stages. There's a trick to affecting not only innocence but broken defiance. There's a tremble in the lips, a shimmer to the eyes, a trick to blinking. I had plenty of opportunities to learn the differences and the techniques. Eddie loved a little power play, and before he could get off he wanted to know he had strained his toy beyond the breaking point.

Joel, however, was a completely different animal than *sigh* Eddie.

"Don't," Joel said. "Don't look at me like that." His cock wilted and he took two quick steps back. "My God," he said, "what am I doing to you?"

"I'm sorry, sir," I said, and that put the final nail in his mood's coffin.

So, Joel wasn't as natural at this as I had believed. Bummer.

Still, my body hummed from everything he had done for me. Oh my, *yes*.

He slumped off to think his modest form of "great thoughts." Guilt hummed sad pop songs in my heart, but the threadbare coat of our union had a silver lining: at least one of us had gotten off.

As I expected, the cops came along to spoil everyone's fun before Sunday. They came in after Joel found the stones to try again, and they found me sucking on his fingers, while he squeezed my breast with his free hand. My captor didn't put up a fight, and they took him away.

Barry lost his oh so important visitation rights when he went up the river. He was a schmuck.

Even Gordon Hewitt, a tycoon who was playing the city council with some falsified contract scheme, got nailed and parked in a barred cell for 10 to 20.

According to the cops, everything ended well and by the book (authored by either Hammett or Chandler, take your pick).

However, I was left broken hearted. Joel and his lovely hands were behind bars. After all the trouble I went to teaching him to tie knots . . . It was not fair. I considered baking him cakes with nail files inside, but doubted he would know what to do with one if he had it.

Nice hands, lousy head.

At least I had Eddie, though. Small hands, but a good head, a nice sense of style and an even better bad attitude. He was my Eagle Scout turned scoundrel. Mmmm.

Still, part of me wonders if I'll never meet the perfect man. Someone who's smart, can tie a good knot, has the spine to be appropriately monstrous and possesses lovely, large hands . . . Is that asking too much?

Cougar's Catch

Hildy lived for Playtime, so when the wide-eyed, not-quite-20-year-old boy sidled up to the bar and flashed his fake ID and ordered a Gray Goose and OJ, she said, "How do you feel about sex on the beach?"

It was a bold opening move, perhaps, but Hildy was getting no younger. The more she thought about Playtime, the more she realised that time was not on her side. She was already 46, and while she was still looking good and still possessed of that youthful energy, soon enough she would have to placate her sexual hungers with men her own age instead of slaking them with someone equally vital.

Of course, the danger to initiating Playtime was discovering if her last encounter was to be truly final, the lingering memory to see her through her golden years.

He was a good-looking kid, clean shaven, in a stylishly patterned white shirt unbuttoned enough to reveal a T-shirt beneath – a gawky-eyed, black and white face belonging to some band called Eraserhead. It was artist couture, the mark of a man with taste enough not to wear only a T-shirt and jeans. At Hildy's question, the boy's cheeks burned with embarrassment – so, at least this guy was not some hardnosed cruiser; his blush response rang as authentic – then when he saw the woman who had asked it – a stunner over twice his age, he blinked a few times and grinned the grin of the perpetually amazed.

When his eyes ran over her, Hildy sat a little straighter. As with any night she visited the tropical & gangster themed Larry's Gin Joint, she was dressed to impress. Tonight she wore a clingy red satin dress that emphasised the curve of her breasts and hips, hair freshly dyed a rich raven black, and contacts that created emeralds from her otherwise sadly dull eyes.

"Sex on the beach?" the young man said. "I've never indulged."

"No?" she flashed him a smile, and he blinked again. Cute response really, though she could grow annoyed if he did not develop any semblance of spine at all. "I'm Hildy," she said. "Are you here for Spring Break?"

"I am," he said. Nicer reply than the "Yeah," she expected. "I'm down from UMadison, where the snow is still thick as, uhm, thick. Miami struck me as a nice spot to wait out the worst."

He had a truly disarming smile when he let it out. It stirred warmth inside her, made parts of her tingle. She eyed him, and watched him puff a little in pride at being eyed. His was a strong body, not quite the tight and pert form of a football player, but certainly not some computer potato MMORPG player. Athletic, a runner's body. This was a guy who liked to take care of himself.

"Oh," he said, with an aw-shucks blush, "I'm Neil."

With another exchange, the initial hello Bee-Ess was done, and Neil's eyes were locked on Hildy's mouth. She had a way of emphasising every O-sound with a subtle sucking motion, making each instance attractive enough to catch Neil's breath, to instil thoughts of what parts he might be able to fit between her lips. She liked things inside as much of her as possible: in her mouth, in her sex, and in her ass. Fingers? She might well love a pair of nice sized fingers inside her mouth while he slid into her from behind. Of course, she might like feeling his hard, young cock in her mouth. That would be nicest yet. She could see him pondering her crouched before him and sucking him off, stroking him with a firm hand and pulling as many gasps and moans from him as possible. Did he imagine her smiling around his lovely shaft while reaching the fingers on her free hand down to rub around her lust swollen clit, to urge herself to tiny ecstasies? Providing Neil was an imaginative enough boy, he would certainly be thinking these things.

"What do you do up there in the snow and the ice?" she asked, to give her mind something to do other than fantasise. She longed to screw her eyes shut, to feel the wonderful friction of his cock head rubbing inside her, tickling the g-spot, drawing moans from the deepest parts of her, building the pressure until it grew too hot.

However, he was not hers yet, and there was no certainty that he would be. Though a part of her mind pondered his performance — would he be a rhythmic lover? Or arrhythmic and annoying? She needed to keep herself occupied so as to avoid possible disappointment.

"I'm a musician," he said. "Studying music theory, I mean. I want to be a composer, like John Williams or Hans Zimmer. Make big sounds for Hollywood."

"How wonderful," she said. He knew a thing or two about maintaining rhythm then.

"Not great money," he said almost apologetically, "except maybe for the lucky handful. As long as I don't turn out like Richard Band or someone, I guess I'll be happy."

The names meant little to her. She eyed him again, noting the way his khakis sat upon his legs, showing muscle not flab. That was a really nice body he was only partially showing. She smiled warmly, teasingly. "I think you'll get by."

"You live around here?" he asked.

"Why, Neil," she said, "You haven't even bought me a drink yet."

"I didn't . . . I mean . . ." His whole face glowed with this blush. "Can I get you something?"

It was then that Larry delivered his Goose and OJ. She held up her mostly empty glass, and Neil said, "That a sex on the beach?" When she nodded, he asked "What's in that?"

"Grenadine, orange juice, pineapple juice, Malibu rum, Peachtree, and a little," she paused to run her tongue across her lip, catching a stray spot of flavour, "cream for smoothness."

"No vodka," he said. "I thought there was Stoli or something."

"Oooh," she said, "a Renaissance man."

"How's that?"

He somehow looked even cuter when confused. She explained, "You are a man of many talents. Music and drink mixes and couture."

"Renaissance man, huh?" He grinned at this and nodded to himself. "I like the sound of that."

"So," she said, "any other talents you'd care to share?"

"A few," he said, and her drink arrived. He slid money across the bar, and the bartender made change while she raised the glass to her lips and tasted. Perfect as usual. Larry knew all about sex and beaches. "Mmm," she said, and then asked "Want a taste?" giving the last word every body language cue of desire she knew.

Still blushing, he said "Sure." She handed the glass over, and when he took it, she brushed across his hand a little longer than necessary. The trick, Hildy knew, was to tease and not come off as desperate. Nothing scared a lovely boy off faster than desperation. She wanted Neil, but she did not want him to know how much she wanted him.

The way he acted was so genuinely intriguing. She could show him a few things, and she could share in his discoveries. Men got off on deflowering virgins, and Hildy got a similar thrill from her catches.

She did not want virgins, per se. She wanted horny lads who knew at least how to find the target when they were naked and ready. She wanted boys with some experience, something past backseat fumbling, past the attempts to apply porn gained theory to the real deed, but not so old that they lost their all night hard-ons.

She crossed her legs at the thought of Neil's hard-on.

Outside of *Desperate Housewives*, American culture worshipped youth to the extent that it seemed a single woman's sex life ended after marriage or 33, whichever happened first. She liked to think this the stuff of nonsense; this being the 21st century, a mature woman should still be able to get plenty of Playtimes. And Playtime with young, happy hard-ons.

Should, however, did not equate to either could *or* would.

"Pretty fucking nice," he said. He could have been talking about drink or her legs. The crotch of those khakis was fuller than when he had arrived, a blossoming hard-on with her name on it, should she play things right. That he had not left yet gave Hildy hope; she only needed to hang on just tight enough to bring him in. Perhaps she had another night's pleasures left in her.

"You think so, huh?" She crossed her legs again, and he took a second sip of her drink. He was relaxed now. She leaned in and touched his leg, high on the thigh, near his cock. "You're pretty fucking nice yourself. You want to get out of here?"

He glanced back, over his shoulder. A table full of friends waited; this was the telling moment: here was where victory or loss would happen. Would Neil flee back to safety of similarly-aged friends or take the plunge for a little play? When he glanced back, she knew his answer even before it passed his lips. This lovely boy was as easy to read as a book, and Hildy had cut her teeth on more challenging texts than bestsellers. Sweet, sweet Neil said, "I'd love to."

How lovely.

"So, you live around here?"

"Not far," she said, "Walking distance. Want to walk with me?"

He said nothing, so she stood and touched his lips with her own, pouring a little more heat into him from her boundless spring. To top it off, she gave his crotch a gentle caress, and he shivered. "Yeah," he said. "Lead on."

It would be simple enough to take him back to her place; she was practically leading him by the cock, as it was. But that would put too quick an end to Playtime. She wanted to savour his affection, to tantalize him just enough but not scare him off. To titillate herself, too. Play went both ways.

Outside, a breeze carried the rich scents of floral displays from the city's recent beautification. In time, they would wilt, they would die and take their scents to the grave. But until then, they were charming enough. The taste of her drink still full on her tongue, she leaned over to kiss Neil again, and his mouth proved as hungry for attention as hers. Gone was the hesitation. His tongue turned tender circles before delving deep into her mouth for a single moment's surprise. Then, it withdrew, an enchanting mix of methods that Hildy found deucedly intoxicating.

When the kiss broke, warm wiggles coursed through her body, starting in her sex but radiating outward. "You're good at that," she said. Boys needed plenty of encouragement.

"Thank you."

She caught his shirt and pulled him down the sidewalk. "Come with me." He seemed to catch that double meaning.

They walked a while, clinging close enough together that she could smell his musk and Axe cologne. Close enough that he could smell her perfume, a naughty, alchemical intoxicant of leather and roses designed to hold a young man's attention. He put his arm low around her waist, so his hand rested along the curve of her ass.

She leaned in against him, letting her own hands run beneath his open shirt, along the Eraserhead logo and the broad chest beneath. His cock continued to strain inside his pants. Every so often they paused to kiss again, and she felt a fresh thrill run through her like electricity.

His hands were on her, too. Clawing her back, leaving trails of heat through her dress or across her bare skin. He was doing his best to undress her on the sidewalk, and his erection nudged her below.

"So," she said between kisses, "Do you have a condom?"

"Yeah," he said.

"Maybe I can't wait," she said, surprising herself, "to get back to my place."

"Here?" His voice trembled with nerves, his expression betrayed perverse intrigue. "In the street?" This particular road saw less foot traffic, though it was still sighting distance to the neon-heavy lane of bars and nightspots. An artery from one stretch of nightlife to the next.

She glanced around. "Maybe not right here," she said, and her eyes passed over the nearby dark doorway to Lawson's Deli. It was a recessed spot, surrounded by shaded glass. The streetlamp light would barely reach inside that recess. "But what about there?"

"There?" The perverse intrigue was winning out, aided no doubt by the demanding cockmind. "Yeah."

She led the way, and as soon as they entered the shadows, he pressed against her. She shoved him back, not the wilting teen flower he might have been with before. "What's wrong?"

"I want you," she said, "to fuck me right."

She pulled her dress down, baring her breasts, and pulled his hands to her hips. Like an obedient boy, he lowered his mouth to suck and nibble. "Not just the nipples," she admonished, "all around." He got the hang of it quick enough, kissing from left to right and back again. "Use your tongue," she whispered, "flick them for me." Each flick brought a new delight.

The glass was cold on her back, but she had heat to spare. Neil's hands caressed her sides, kneading her with intensifying eagerness. She tugged up his T-shirt, while his mouth sent shivers through her. Could he smell her yet? The hot honey lubricant flowing below was strong in her nostrils.

"Kiss my mouth," she said. He was born to serve.

"Along the neck," she said. "Now, bite my shoulder." The boy's mouth was spectacular. His hands moved up to massage her breasts and occasionally flick her nipples. "Pinch them," she said. "Harder." He squeezed her and she trembled. Her lip found its way between her teeth and she ground it near to bursting. "Oh, Neil. What a bad boy you are."

That set him off even more. He redoubled his nibbles and kisses, his talented tongue tricks, his hands.

She reached low, unzipped him, and manoeuvred his cock into her palm. The soft skin bent to the right, a pleasurable size, not too wide. No socks stuffed down these shorts to compensate for perceived inadequacies.

She stroked it; her tight grip delivered gasps. "Too hard?" she asked, knowing that he would not say no. He would only shake his head to the negative. "Harder?" She squeezed him a little more, milking his ecstasy. "Such a fine, big cock," she said, and when he glanced up, she licked her lips. "Where's your condom?"

He fumbled for his wallet. Dropped it. Cursed between gasps. "I'll get it," she said, and slowly sank to her knees, stroking his lovely cock as she dropped. Her dress and skin squeaked down the glass, as she went.

His wallet came to hand and she stuffed it into his palm, gazing at the prize in her fist. The head was lovely, dotted with lubricant. So close. Kissably close. She longed to taste him, to feel that soft skin on her tongue, to feel it move when she sucked. Finally he fumbled the condom out.

Non-lubricated.

Perfect.

She dragged it out of his hand, ripped it open and set it in place. Squeezed the tip and unrolled it over his glans. Then, she leaned in and set her lips along the latex, pushing forward, unrolling the rest of the way with her mouth. Neil was all aquiver, so he must have liked what she was doing. She hummed late Beatles tunes, and he rocked back, catching himself on the deli door.

When his cock tickled the back of her throat, it caught enough of a gag reflex to draw forth plenty of saliva. The latex taste was bad, but not enough to turn her off sucking him. She wrapped a hand around his sheathed cock, stroking him, while she sucked. He writhed against the door, just as she wanted him to.

Then, she reached into his pants and squeezed his balls. They were shaved and goose pimpled. He whispered her name like a prayer, and she found she liked it. *Worship me*, she thought. *Love me.*

One of his hands moved down to play with her hair, while the other reached into his gaping shirt to flick his own nipple. Nice to see a man who was not afraid to pleasure himself.

She reached down and tugged her panties aside, so trembling fingers might rub circles around her throbbing clit, drawing along either side and then across. Her first orgasm hit when she glanced up and saw Neil's boyish handsome face twisting delightfully from in her attentions. The cock in her mouth muffled her verbalization, but the energy crashed through her. Buoyant with joy, she tugged harder on his cock and fingered herself.

"I want you inside me," she said. She stood, tugged down her panties and pulled up her dress.

He was all hands, now, intoxicated with the scent of desire. At least he showed enough reserve that he did not simply bludgeon her with his attention. She leaned back against the glass and spread her legs. The window was cold on her ass, but this sensation only got her hotter still. A hold on his cock allowed her to guide the head to her slit. She smiled up at him, seeing the urge to plough into her. "A little at first, OK?"

He got into it, especially when she hooked her left leg around him. "More now." His cock spread her slowly. "All the way, Neil,' she said.

He shook his head. "Not yet." He moved slowly in and out, giving her almost an inch at a time. So nice. His cock felt so good, spreading her, pushing inside her. A gentle rubbing, no friction at all. She found herself moaning through a second orgasm when he was still an inch or so away from being fully inside her. Her fingernails caught the back of his neck, and her leg tightened around him. Her skin squeaked across the glass as it left warm prints.

She whispered that she was coming, ordered him not to stop, don't you dare stop. To the contrary, Neil was just getting going. He sank as deeply into her as possible, filling her. Then he was out again. In. He built tempo. Orchestrated her gasps and moans like music. Composing a symphony of her satisfaction and conducting that sheet music like an expert. "Harder," she pleaded, "Fast–"

He was in sync with her desires, and his cock moved faster now. He shoved into her, unapologetic and rough. The glass was hard, and the back of her head rapped across it twice. He was stabbing her, now, berserk with lust, and she lost all sense of where they were. There was only the wonderful rubbing, only the flow. He was fucking her and saying her name, and she was basking in his attention, in his glorious cock and hands and kisses and . . . She came again, and leaned forward to clamp his nipple between her teeth. He bucked at this, moaning some pain, some pleasure, and as she sucked him, she growled for him to come too. To come for *her*. To come *inside* her.

His cock stiffened as his pleasure burst forth, and he whimpered a little as the sensitivity hit him.

She looked into his face, sweet in the moments after. He was smiling, pleased with himself. She reached up to caress his cheek, and her bracelets clinked like denouement cymbals.

Without her leg around him, Neil leaned back, his shrivelling cock falling out of her. The condom hung from his drooping member like some strange, pendulous wattle.

She rearranged her dress, pulling it down over her ass and up across her breasts, and he said, "Damn that was fun." An element of disappointment that the night was done.

"A lot of fun," she said. "And, honey, I'm game if you want to come over, rest up and try a little more."

In the dark, she could tell he was blinking while he thought. She could see the subtle movement as he shifted his head to look back to Larry's and his forgotten friends. He was thinking with a clearer head, and it was anyone's guess if he would cut and run on her.

"I think I'd love that," he said.

The cougar led him further on, enjoying the afterglow, the night, and her sweet catch. What would tomorrow hold? She would not say, but tonight was perfectly lovely.

Sexual Appetites

Monday night at Grace's Seven, the poshest wine tasting bar on the Northwest side of San Antonio, was karaoke night, a time for the harshest renditions of Hank Williams, Johnny Cash, and Cowboy Troy imaginable. One drunk cowboy after another took the mic and belted out their heartfelt, wine flavored best. I was the DJ, and I'll be honest when I confess I dreaded karaoke. The regular gig paid the bills, though. And Danny behind the bar was good with all the glasses of zin I could drink—the Good Stuff, not Zin from an el cheapo box.

During a lull, the blonde walked up to my table, nervous but fresh faced and excited. She was a pretty thing, my pal Ryan would call her "a little on the heavy side" when he was sober or "a Queen-Sized Gal" when drunk, but I paid this little detail no never mind. More woman to love, so far as I figured. A nametag from some Event she had just escaped adhered over her left breast, with a typed "Hi, I'm" and a purple Sharpie scribbled "CLARA."

"You got a lot of songs, Mr. Dugan Rocks," she said, glancing toward the binder. She had not even opened it yet.

"That I do, Clara, right?"

Surprise and suspicion colored her face, until she realized she was wearing the nametag. "Oops, geek badge," she said, and tore it off.

"You're no cowgirl," I said. "What do you do for a living?"

"Nutritionist," she said. "Food science research with UTSCA." The University of Texas branch of the South Texas Medical Center. "We had a St. Patty's potluck and mixer." She waved to the binder. "You really have ten thousand songs?"

"Sure do."

"How would I pick one from that big old book?"

"You have any favorites? You don't need to flip pages. There's a whole hellovalot in the computer. Request away . . ."

"You have Alhanna Myles? 'Black Velvet'?"

"I do indeed." It was an undeniably sexy little number, one I dreaded hearing butchered on a night like this. "You're up in three," I said, and added her name to my dry erase board. Her smile filled her face, and she said, "Thanks!" and I couldn't help but smile too. She had a glow. Her beauty reminded me of my first gal, Suzy Sommerfeld, a sexy little brunette who showed me more ways to tie a tongue than I ever imagined in the back seat of my Daddy's 72 Chevy . . . This Clara shared an earnestness with Suzy, a real "set your sights and go for it" attitude.

When she got up to sing, I let the thrum of the music move through me and steeled myself for ostrich squawks. Damned if she didn't squawk even once. She had the husky bluesy sex sound down perfect. Everyone in the Seven gazed at her a while, as she transformed from a chubby gal to a smoldering sexpot songbird. Then the song faded out, and Clara flashed me that smile, and I gave her a thumbs up, and I thought that was that.

Before the end of my set, she asked if she could buy me a drink. "Let me share one with you," I said, "since I'm comped." We sat together a while and sipped zin and talked. Really talked, and she showed a whole other side. *In vino veritas* is the unofficial motto of Grace's Seven, and that's high fallutin' for "There's Truth in Wine."

We talked a lot, and I found myself increasingly turned on. She was smart and funny, and honest, not afraid to admit that she had something of an addictive personality: though her addictions ran to confectionaries rather than the harder candies.

"Well look at us," I said, "two gluttons finding each other in San Antonio."

"You?" she said. She was looking at me, then. At the way I was now, gym slim and weight lifted toned.

"Me," I said. "Lost almost one hundred pounds over the last three years," I said, and made a muscle, and she smiled and touched it. Her face flushed, and I sensed an echo of my own arousal. "But you know what I like more than anything?"

"What's that?" she said.

"Getting a mess of popcorn," I said, "and sharing it with someone while the last picture show of the night plays."

She blushed.

"You like that too, huh?"

"Want to share," she said, "some popcorn with me?" I imagined reaching into the bucket in her lap, and said, "Sure." And that was how we ended up at the Alamo Drafthouse, sharing a tub of popcorn and better kisses than were on screen. The movie was negligible; give me Jeff Bridges rugged over Russell Crowe polish any day. . .

Carol kissed really well. The kind of kisses make a man forget all about such trivialities like time. Don't quite know where the popcorn went, but our hands moved around each other, hungry to bare skin, to share the fire. With every kiss, I craved her more and more.

Her skin was soft to the touch, powdered. She reached up under my shirt, and tweaked my nipples, and the sensation hit me like lightning. "I want you," I said. "Will you come home with me?"

"I will," she said, before she sucked on my tongue and tweaked my nipple again, sending lusty lightning racing down to my cock, and I said forget the picture show, let's get the hell going.

My place was a small apartment off Medical Drive, near the hospital center. We kissed our way through the front door, and we giggled when I knocked into everything. I drew her to the couch, and she pulled up her shirt, and I saw plenty of beautiful skin in need of some kisses and nibbles and licks. Her sports bra hid two lovely, full breasts, and I looked forward to tweaking her nipples for a little luscious payback.

"You got anything to drink?" she asked.

Of course, I did, and when I fetched a bottle of Cab-Merlot, she ignored the glasses and poured the liquor down my chest. Cleaned out my belly button and then drank it from there. She poured a shot into her mouth, and fed it to me while we kissed. The liquor spilled down my front, and I'll be damned if I wasn't even more aroused.

"Like it?" she asked, before taking a hit of the stuff for herself.

"Do I." An idea struck me. "Wait'll you see this." I fetched some chocolate sauce I'd been saving for a special occasion. Spurted a little on my finger, and rubbed it around her lips before I kissed her again. The sticky syrup's sweetness mixed with the wine in delicious ways. Adding pheromones made a heady intoxicant, indeed.

I dribbled the cold sauce in a trail up her legs to her sex, and licked my way to her pussy. As my tongue rubbed around her clitoris, the chocolate sweetness mingled with her body's iron flavor in unexpected ways. I drooled for her, kissing her to climax after climax. She dragged me up by my hair and our tongues met, and she purred as aftershocks make her quiver.

The stickiness made lovemaking strange, almost brand new. Familiar sensations were skewed just enough to make us feel like virgins all over again, and the love we made—starting slow and sassy, moving too fast fucking and back—sent shivers of pleasure through us. She was a verbalizer, a dirty talker, and the things she said drove me further faster.

Then, she rolled me onto my back and ate chocolate off of me.

Appetites for food, appetites for sex. For us, there was no difference. We were both eating each other in a chocolate sauce sixty nine. She gagged on my banana shaft, while I buried face and nose in her slit. Her thighs clamped around my head and we both gasped in unison.

Her climaxes dribbled from my chin like chowder, when I sheathed in latex and mounted her from behind. She moaned as I pulled her onto my cock with steady, strong hands. With her sassy dirty talk, I swelled even larger. She came, again, and pounding the cushions as she did so, and soon it was too much for me, and I filled my condom. My cock twitched inside her like a conductor's baton signaling the start of the orchestral number.

We collapsed beside each other, spooning and giggling and talking about next time.

Next time?

We'd already planned to do it again. With food.

Just like that, we were both addicted.

The next night, we discovered how body play with props can be even hotter than either of us ever believed. We emptied my fridge.

Ice chips rubbed on certain sensitive places at the right time are amazing stimulators. Berries fill niches, squirting sticky juice when squeezed beneath palm or lips. Whipped cream made a sundae of a body. Peanut butter was nice and thick and left its flavors long after the dollop was gone . . .

At her place, on Wednesday, we delved into more unusual flavors, smearing tomato sauce and spraying a little Cheez in a Can. We gobbled each other, hungrier yet. The sex was intense. She orgasmed dozens of times, before I finally climaxed. Even then, we nibbled sweets, adding flavor to our kisses.

Thursday, Friday, Saturday. We'd go out to dinner together, make the act of eating sexy. Seductions accompanied by forks and knives. Our lives were food and sex, sex and food, and let me tell you, we had a blast!

Until I discovered the bad news, Sunday morning. All that fucking was not compensating for the calories. I was a couple pounds up. What did it matter, though? The sex was hot, the food was tasty. I could triple my gym workouts, maybe. Did celery have a sexual use?

I was game to try.

What were the sexual uses for pumpkins? We would find out (not much, alas), but the weight kept coming. End of the following week, I was up ten pounds, little of it useful muscle.

"We need to talk," I said at our third karaoke meeting. She had just finished singing "Lollypop," complete with finger pulled from her cheek pop sound effects. "I need to cut back a little."

"Cut back?" Had I slapped her, she might not have been more startled. "Cut back on what?"

"Well, the food is . . ." I rubbed a hand over my growing belly. "It's having a way with me."

"You want to stop?"

"No," I said. "But I need to figure out something." I leaned close to say, "I love when we're together, but I don't want to backslide too far."

"Oh," she said, in that way that told me she understood my words in a way I had not intended.

"Wait," I said. "I'm just thinking of shifting to more on the fruit side, less on the processed side."

"The stuff I suggested?"

"I brought out the chocolate first," I said.

She considered this and nodded, and then walked up to the bar where Danny had a glass of chardonnay ready for her. She didn't talk to me the rest of the night. In fact, she took off before my set was done, and she didn't answer her phone when I called.

That was it, I thought. Over and done.

Made me sad. That gal was a real sweetie. The kind to give a man cavities.

#

She showed up on my doorstep Wednesday night, wearing a long coat and carrying a courier bag. "Hey Dugan Rocks. You really got ten thousand songs on your hard drive?"

"Indeed, I do." I smiled to see her, and she gave me that big old, beautiful grin of hers. "I was afraid you'd left me high and dry, Clara."

"Well, maybe I was a little hurt that night, but I got to thinking . . . Thinking maybe you were right. I've never been all the way good about myself. Eating is kind of my Achilles Heel."

"And you thought I was insulting you," I said. It made a kind of sense. Not a whole lot, but enough that I didn't want to push it too hard. "Come on in."

She did, and then she opened the bag, and I saw a bunch of low fat food in there. Sugar free. "Well, look at that," I said.

"I usually hate diet food," she said. "But I'm willing to give these a go. Maybe there'll be something we both like."

I took her in my arms. "Darling," I said, "I already see something I like just fine."

She wasn't wearing much under that coat. And soon enough, we were both wearing a lot less.

Sugar free peanut butter is pretty good, so long as you remember to mix in a little sugar substitute. Vanilla yogurt is surprising, too. Prunes leave a sticky juice that invites some serious sucking, though they should be used sparingly. Trust me on this.

For my money, sugar free chocolate sauce should be jettisoned from the face of the planet. Nothing more vile than that.

For all our good times, it was inviting to be naughty and go for the real stuff, non-diet chocolate. Sometimes to be good, we all need to be a little bad: It makes life and love all the . . . sweeter.

Hush Hush, My Love, and Thank You

The finest hospital care for wounded soldiers could be found in San Antonio, so when Sgt. Joe Givens' wife and family found out he had been flown to Fort Sam Houston, they took it as a good sign. A smart young woman in uniform met Molly Givens at the airfield with good news delivered like bullet points: Joe was in the best possible hands, Joe was no longer in critical care, and Joe was likely to have at least partial mobility back after the reconstructive surgeries and physical therapy. The smart soldier's nametag read Leonard.

As they walked to the car, Molly asked, "How bad was the damage, Corporal Leonard?" because she could not ask "How much of my husband has come home?"

"I really can't say."

"You don't know, or you can't answer 'in an official capacity'? I don't mind an off the record warning of what I'm walking into."

After a moment's consideration, the Corporal said, "I won't lie. It was pretty extensive. I didn't get many details, but I got that much. Still, the prognosis is good."

"I've heard Fort Sam has great healthcare."

"And they're working wonders with titanium and bone transplants," Corporal Leonard added before a look of *ERROR ERROR* flashed across her face. "My God, I'm so sorry."

"No apologies. I'm knew the risks when I married a military man. I . . . . I told myself this could happen." She had just never expected it.

"He's in the best possible hands."

Molly spent the rest of the ride in silence. She thought about her happiest times, and the best revolved around intimacy with Joe.

#

The first time they had made love, Molly and Joe had not shared last names. It was the evening after their senior prom, and Molly—then Brownfinkle—had been wearing a black and teal taffeta gown, her auburn hair drawn up and held in place with decorative chopsticks. Joe had been tugging at the collar and cuffs on his rented tux all night. The only part he seemed comfortable with was the teal cummerbund, but damn he looked good. Their class colors were not quite gag-puke awful, but in the motel after the dance, she was glad to get rid of the clothes.

He helped her—fumbled with her more like. They were both virgins. She had planned she would remain one until her wedding night. Then, she had met this handsome fellow and concluded waiting was not necessary. This guy would be around for her, no matter what Momma said about "all men." Joe was reliable.

And his butt looked damned good in jeans.

But tonight, he was not wearing jeans. Soon enough, he was not wearing anything but a shy smile. His body was a gorgeous sculpture. Tight muscles and a six pack. He was a hot guy who didn't know just how hot he was. Or else he downplayed it on purpose.

She taught him how to touch her. His fingertips were rough, his palms soft. When they massaged her breasts they started too hard, then got too gentle when she said "Ow." She guided him toward just right, and he was a fast learner.

His cock fascinated her. It looked kind of like a skinny butternut squash and rose at a steep angle. At the end grew a glistening tear. It was softer than she expected, and she held it too hard, and then too gentle when *he* said "Ow." They laughed together, which killed some tension.

She had not counted on so much tension being there. Sure, it had built up inside her during the long wait for this moment. A part of her hoped it would vanish when she saw him naked. When she saw how he looked at her with love and lust mixed.

He was a good kisser. She liked the way their tongues moved together, liked the way he invaded her mouth, liked the way he held her close when he did. His cock nudged her, impatient for action.

She said, "Do you have a condom?" One waited in her purse if needed; *not an invitation*, she assured herself, *a precaution*.

He did. A gray packaged Trojan. Ultra-thin, the package said. With spermicidal lubricant.

She watched him tear the packet open. The condom looked so fragile in his big hands. But watching him slide it down his shaft was intensely erotic.

They lay on the bed together. She spread her legs and he settled between them. They shivered together. His cock misaligned and a thrust sent it up between her labia instead of in. It must've felt good, because he kept rubbing. "Wait," she said, and reached down to guide him in. The condom rubber felt funny, cool to the touch and flimsy. Not at all like her vibrator.

She guided him in, felt his flares notch, and then he thrust. There was pain, but not as much as she had thought there would be. There was discomfort, but not as much as she expected. There was a surprising connectedness.

Their first time was not their best, but it was their first.

He thrust six, seven times before he came. Then, he lay atop her, panting and sweating, and he said, "I love you."

Her voice caught in her throat, and her eyes filled with tears and she felt a blubbering idiot, but it was a nice moment. A really nice moment.

"Hush, hush, my love," he said. After a heartbeat's worth of silence, he added, "And thank you." She told him not to thank her because girls don't want to feel like soup kitchens. They laughed some more, and his cock shriveled inside the condom inside her.

She held onto him and cried a while and then he told her he was considering skipping college. "Only for a little while. I'm considering joining the army. Maybe become a Ranger, if they'll have me."

She cried some more.

Then, he asked her if she wanted to, you know, maybe stay together a while? They were already steady, so that could only mean . . .

And she cried some more and said, "Yes, Joe. Yes, yes, yes."

#

At Fort Sam Houston, Corporal Leonard guided Molly to the office of a Dr. Dwayne Tan, a Hawaiian man with sensitive eyes, round cheeks and a captain's rank. Tan offered her a seat and a box of tissues. "I want to prepare you, Mrs. Givens." In his mid-thirties, he seemed far too young to be a doctor.

"Captain, can you tell me what happened?"

"Many details about the operation remain classified," Tan said. "What I do know is this. During routine transport duties, an IED detonated under Joe's truck outside Mosul. Shrapnel penetrated through the vehicle floor, resulting in incredible damage to Joe's legs, arms and torso."

"My God."

"Despite the intense agony he must have been in, Joe Givens continued to operate the vehicle, preventing its turning over and guiding it away from an ambush."

"He did all that?"

Dr. Tan nodded. "There are at least five men who owe him their lives."

"Were they all wounded like Joe?"

"All wounded, yes," Tan said. "But Joe sustained the worst damage."

"That's my G. I. Joey," she said, taking three tissues from the box with quick wrist flicks.

"He's a courageous young man, Mrs. Givens."

"Can I see him?"

"You can," Tan said. "But I want to make you aware of the situation. Things are going to look, well, they will look impossible. We've made incredible advances in reconstructive technologies, even over the last ten years—"

"I understand," she said, tired of the reassurances. "I want to see my husband."

#

On their wedding night, Molly and Joe had been exhausted, happy and a little drunk—both on the Dom her parents had insisted upon and on the wonderful whirlwind experience of saying "I do" followed by never quite sitting down at the reception. She had fallen into his arms, and laughter flowed like bubbles in the champagne.

This had been the second time she had seen him in a tuxedo, and he cleaned up so well. On leave after basic, head covered with stubble instead of the shoulder length sandy falls she enjoyed grabbing onto. Rubbing his head was like touching velvet—move from face to rear and the experience was nice enough, but try to move in reverse at your peril.

They had made love twenty-seven times between prom and marriage. She had hoped for more, but enjoyed what she got. Each was better than the last as they learned what their bodies wanted and could accomplish.

Their wedding night shared trappings with prom. Molly once more wore too much taffeta and they were pawing at each other in another hotel room. This time, the dress was off-white and the room was at the top of the Noble Building, downtown, classier than the post-prom motel Joe had managed to book.

In the morning, they would be flying to sunny NoCal to spend a trio of days in shiny San Francisco. The hotel there promised a great view of the bridge and the bay. She imagined wine country would be a dark smear near the horizon.

However, the wedding night was the wedding night, and not to be overlooked for the honeymoon. They stripped to underwear—he beheld her wedding lingerie with an open mouth and unblinking eyes—and sat on the big bed together, holding each other and whispering the silly nothings, which meant everything, and giggling and kissing. His tongue tasted like Dom and too much frosting. His body was already sweating from the dance floor, but it was a clean sweat.

He was even more toned, now. A military man with a future and she was now an Army bride, which sounded okay with her. Scary, but okay.

No longer Mrs. Brownfinkle, now she was Givens.

And he was givens her as hard a time as he could. Joe was a punny guy, and the best way to stop the endless assaults on the

English language was to kiss him. To touch him. To pull his hands to her bustier and then up to her breasts.

Joe's strong hands massaged her, while he kissed, licked and nibbled his way from her mouth down her throat and further. Her nipples were painfully erect when his mouth closed over the left. His teeth and tongue teased her, and she moaned for him to take her, please. Now, please.

He said, "Want to try something?"

What his hands were accomplishing urged her to say, "Yes," without knowing the particulars. She resisted enough to say, "What?" Resistance made things a little more intense.

"How about I tie you up?"

Tie her up? For years, her fantasies had revolved around restraints. Too embarrassed to say anything, she had made do with fantasy life, fucking her vibrator while calling his name while daydreaming about he might bind her with scarves or stockings. "I'd like that a lot."

He was a boy scout—always prepared. In his luggage, he had four ten-foot lengths of rope. Silky, he assured her, not rough. They were colorful, interwoven purple and black strands. He laid these on the bed. Molly picked one up. They were softer than she expected but still, well, *ropy*.

"Neat," she said.

He lifted her, and she giggled. Though she was one hundred sixty pounds, he plucked her off the bed like she was a doll. Laid her so her head was on the pillows. His smile was playful when he wrapped a rope around one wrist. The line was snug, not pinching, when he pulled it taut and tied it to the headboard. He repeated this trick, tucking the lines under the loops to keep them from squeezing the hell out of her. The sensation was unbelievably erotic, safe and secure and oh my God, she was his prisoner.

He could do anything he wanted with her.

Judging from their previous encounters, she liked the things that came to his mind.

"This feels incredible," she said, and then whooped when he caught her ankles and pulled her down the bed. She giggled, when her arms went taut. He tied each ankle to the frame. She was spread-eagle, her flooding desire filling her nostrils.

"You look delicious," he said, "and you smell divine."

"What now?" she asked.

"Let me worship you awhile." He knelt between her legs and kissed her from ankles to knee and higher. His teeth nibbled inside her thighs and she gasped. His hands kneaded her flesh while he kissed her through her panties. Silk made those kisses softer. Her pussy overflowed. She whispered his name like a mantra.

The mantra changed when he pulled her panties aside, and used his lips and tongue on her. Mantra became passion-song. His fingers played inside while his tongue turned sexy circles around her clit. Too much, so good, oh no—

She came at his touch, amazed it had happened so fast.

He was not done, however. His mouth kept at her. She trembled, whispering for him to wait a minute, give her a chance to recover, but he did not. The sensation was not painful, but a bit uncomfortable, and then she was through the discomfort and returning to pleasure.

His mouth made her come once more before he climbed her like a ladder. His cock bobbed before her face, and he took it in hand. "Suck on my balls," he said. It was an invitation, one she might refuse if she chose, not that she ever wanted to. She took his testicles in her mouth, sucking on them while he moaned and played with his shaft.

Her hands turned in the ropes, tugging against them. They held her firm. Unyielding.

It was amazing, how easily she slipped into the role. There was no fear, no hesitation. This was Joe, after all. Her Joe. Lover. Boyfriend. Husband, now.

She sucked him until he pulled out, red faced and gasping.

"Fuck me," she said. "Now."

Strange to be giving orders from the bound position. Still, he listened. Moved between her legs and entered her without guidance.

She was wet beyond belief, but the sensation was still amazing. He filled her so well and so deep. It was all him, too. No rubber in the way. No condom interference. She felt closer to him than she imagined anyone could feel to another person.

She came on him after five thrusts. Then, he fucked her harder. *Yes*. Faster. *Yes*. And then she came again. *Yesyesyes*.

He squeezed his eyes shut. "Molly, I'm going to . . . going to . . ."

"Yes," she said, "come in me. Please come in me."

And he did.

They lay together, afterward, sweating and panting together as the heat they built together ebbed.

"Amazing," she whispered. She meant his hands and mouth and, yes, his cock. She also meant more than these. It was his heart she loved the most. His spirit. His warrior's determination. His will.

In the end, he looked into her eyes and said the seven words that made her laugh. Their little post coital ritual:

"Hush hush, my love. And thank you."

She did not swat him until after he let her out of the ropes.

#

She almost turned away when she recognized him. He looked so different, a tiny lump under the sheets in the bed attended by rubber tubes and wires and machines. The thick bandages on his face made him look emaciated. His one uncovered eye was too wet. But it was him.

Dear sweet lord, it was her Joe.

Her vision swam with tears she refused to shed, until he said, "Hiya, sweet pea."

"I'm sorry," she said as the tears ran. "I'm sorry."

Tam's tissue box was a lifesaver. She pulled one out, used it and realized she still stood outside the privacy sheet's track, looking in. Move, she told her legs, but they did not want to.

"It's okay, honey," he said. Still strong, still trying to take care of her.

My god, he's missing so much. How can he still be so damned strong?

"You don't have to stay," he said. This was when she discovered the quaver in his voice. He wanted her to stay. He needed her the way she had needed him so many times before.

This desperation, this *need* pushed, pulled, shoved, drew her in. Her movements felt stiff, but she walked to the plastic, vinyl and steel chair. She sat beside her man and stared into his face and took his hand and though the tears still fell, she said, "I love you, Joey. I'm not going anywhere. I'm staying with you."

He moaned with relief. "All the way home," he said, "I was so afraid you'd just leave me. See the half-thing who came home and think he wasn't the man you married. I was so afraid, Moll. So afraid."

"It's scary," she said. "No lie there. And they say it won't be easy. But I'm here, baby. I'm here for as long as you need me. I need you too, you know."

"I wish I'd never signed up."

She let him talk a while, let him cry, let him feel sorry for himself until she couldn't stand it anymore. "Stop it, Joe. You signed up because you believed. You still do. And if you hadn't been there, those men with you . . . They'd be dead."

His eye blinked. "They're alive?"

"They're alive because of you."

It was something for him to hold on to. That and her hand gave him a base to touch, a foundation to rebuild from. The determination was all his own. He asked her an eleven word question she did not know the answer to:

"Will we ever Hush Hush, My Love, and Thank You again?"

That question hung in the air between them, a wall too high to scale. Finally, she said, "I will find out."

Hours passed by his side. At Joe's insistence, she spent the night in a hotel instead of beside his bed. "But I want to stay with you," she said.

"And I want you to be a hell of a lot more comfortable than I am," he replied. "I'm not going anywhere. I'll be here tomorrow."

A joke? Though neither a beloved pun nor a knee slapper, it was the first joke he had tried to tell. It had to mean something.

She made it a point to run into Dr. Tan on her way out.

"You're a tough lady," he said. "Joe's a lucky man."

"Doctor, can I ask you a question? Joe asked, and I'm curious."

"Certainly."

"Will he and I ever make love again?"

He asked, "Won't you sit down?" and she wanted to die inside. How was she going to tell Joe?

She said, "Oh God, no."

"It's not as bad as that." Still, Tan guided her to another uncomfortable chair. "The odds are good, but it's going to take time and quite a bit of surgery. However, it's unknown if Joe will ever be able to father children."

"We can't," she said, "have them, anyway. I'm . . ." She clutched her belly when she found herself unable to say the word "infertile," so she repeated, "We can't have them, anyway."

"You have to join with me," Tan said. "Believe Joe will make a recovery. We're doing everything we can, but we need him to keep believing. And that means you—"

"I believe in him," she said. "And I believe in us. And I have to believe in you. You'll do everything, right? Everything you can?"

"I swear I will."

"We're doing all we can," she said, wiping her face dry. "So I expect nothing less from you."

"Joe's a lucky man," Tan said.

"I will see you tomorrow, Doctor. And the next tomorrow. Until Joe is better, back on top again. And Doctor?"

"Yes, Mrs. Givens?"

"Don't you be Givens us any hard times, okay?"

Tan looked confused until she smiled, then he realized it was safe to chuckle. "I won't."

"Good, Doctor. And thank you in advance."

#

The next time he posed that eleven word question again, erecting that wall once more between them, she reached between the bricks made from doubt, anger and fear, and she took his hand in hers. Laced their fingers together. Squeezed, firmly but not painfully. The simple gesture spoke a lot.

It said, *I believe we will.*

It said, *it won't be easy.*

It said, *we are worth the effort.*

It said, *some day soon I hope to wrap this hand around another part of you.*

It said, *hush hush, my love.*

It said, *and thank you.*

Joe wept quietly, and she joined him. The road ahead was dark, and it was fraught with agony. However, a light shone further down, twinkling for the both of them, whispering reassurances, whispering their names.

About the Author

Kaysee Renee Robichaud has been publishing her erotica and romantic fiction since 2008, through such well-known book publishers as Circlet Press, Ravenous Romance, Cleis and Alyson Books. Her work has appeared in numerous anthologies, including the Lambda Award finalist Women of the Bite, edited be Cecilia Tan. An audio version of her story "Adrift" appeared as episode 226 of the Nobilis podcast.

Kaysee Renee has lived all over the United States, but currently resides in southern Texas, where the winters are actually a lot like her childhood autumns. The summers, though, are pretty rough. She is eternally grateful for air conditioning, though a little sweat is good for the fiction.

Keep up with her blog at: http://kayseerenee.livejournal.com/.